An Alien Spring

by
Anne Schraff

Perfection Learning Corporation
Logan, Iowa 51546

Cover: Doug Knutson

Printed in the U.S.A.

20 PP 08 07 06

1

IT HAD BEEN a strange spring right from the beginning. Two tornadoes came howling down in February and four people were killed. Nobody had ever seen anything like it. A big, black funnel cloud sucked everything up into the air. Some people said it wasn't a regular tornado. They said tornadoes in February were unnatural.

Then there were those lightning storms. The thunder roared like a hundred jet engines. Old-timers said there had never been such lightning storms.

But the most frightening event—at least for teenager Mark Scott—came one early March night. As Mark lay in bed, he suddenly heard a terrible whining sound. It sounded like a scream. It was so loud it made his ears ache.

Mark leaped out of bed and ran to the window. It was two in the morning. Yet Mr. Velliers' cornfield next door looked as though it were standing in full sunlight. Something was glowing in the cornfield—something incredibly bright.

"Mom! Dad!" Mark shouted as he ran

down the hall. "Wake up, quick! Something really strange is happening in Mr. Velliers' cornfield!"

As Mark ran through the house, the thought of all those tornadoes and lightning storms came to his mind. Maybe the old-timers were right. Maybe there was something unnatural about the weather.

Mark, along with his younger sister, Grace, and his parents, ran to the Velliers' farm. It was about a quarter of a mile away. By the time they got there, most of the cornfield had already burnt. Mr. Velliers and his grandson Hugh were standing there, ready to take action in case the fire kicked up again.

"Did a plane crash?" Mark's father asked.

Mr. Velliers scratched his thick white hair. "Can't figure what happened. Just heard a terrible roar. I came out here and everything was burning. Just seemed to blaze up."

The last flames began to die down. Soon there was nothing left but ashes and some swirling smoke.

"Look," Grace said, "there's a dent in the ground."

Mark looked hard. Sure enough, the ground was caved in near the center of the fire. "Maybe a meteor landed," he said.

"Don't see any meteor," Mr. Velliers said. "I don't like it. Just seems like a funny thing. Big hole in the ground. Fire coming from nowhere. I don't like it."

"Maybe a flying saucer landed," Grace giggled. "You know, one of those UFOs." Grace was fourteen and had curly brown hair. She also had a wild imagination.

Hugh laughed. "There's no such thing as flying saucers!"

But Mr. Velliers didn't laugh. "I don't like it," he said again. "It isn't right. I'm an old man. I've seen plenty of strange stuff. But I've never seen anything like what's been happening around here lately. Just don't like it."

Everyone drifted home then, but for days people talked about what had happened.

Later on in the week, some experts

came to investigate. They took soil samples and hurried away.

"Maybe those guys were from the Air Force," Grace said. "They investigate UFOs, don't they?"

Mark nodded. "They used to. It was called Project Blue Book. But they decided UFOs weren't real."

Mark was sixteen, and he had always been interested in scientific things. He wasn't sure if he believed UFOs really existed or not.

On Monday, Mark sat next to Bill Bryant on the bus. Bill was in many of the same classes as Mark, and he and Mark were both on the basketball team.

"Did you see the Marnard *Tribune*?" Bill asked. "They had a funny article about little green men and flying saucers."

"Yeah. Sure is weird though—that big hole right in the middle of the cornfield."

Then they began talking about basketball and Ms. Armstrong's chemistry test coming up that day.

As they talked, Mark watched the flat,

dreary countryside fly by the bus windows. Sometimes he wished for mountains or even hills. It was pretty dull in the prairie town of Marnard. Only seven hundred people lived there and nothing very exciting ever happened. Maybe that was why the strange tornadoes and the fire at Velliers' had made such an impression on everybody.

Mark and Bill walked into chemistry together. They both saw the new boy at the same moment. He had blue-black hair and eyes the color of turquoise. He stared straight ahead without looking at anybody.

A girl leaned toward Mark when he sat down. "The new guy is deaf."

"Yeah?" Mark said.

"Uh-huh. I was in the office this morning when he came in. Ms. Brent told me."

Mark sympathized with the new guy. Starting at a new school was never easy. It could be even worse if people tended to ignore you because they thought you were different. Mark decided he would try to help the guy find his way around.

"Our new student is Edward Thomas," Ms. Armstrong explained before the quiz. "He lip-reads, so face him when you talk to him. And please make him feel welcome at our school."

The quiz wasn't as bad as Mark had anticipated. After the bell, he rushed to catch up with Edward. He touched the boy's arm to make him turn. Then he smiled and said, "Hi, I'm Mark Scott. Welcome to Marnard High. I hope you'll like it here."

Edward did not smile; he just stared. He gripped his books with large, wide hands. Mark had never seen such large hands. The boy's clothing was strange, too. It didn't fit him. His shirt was too long and his jeans were too short.

After pausing for a moment, Edward hurried away from Mark and disappeared around a corner.

Bill joined Mark. "Did you talk to him?" he asked.

"I tried to. But I think I blew it. I scared the poor guy," Mark said sadly.

Bill shook his head. "He looks weird—

you know, retarded—to me."

Mark felt anger rising in him. "That's stupid!" he shouted. Right away he knew he shouldn't have yelled. Yet he couldn't help it. Last fall his dad had had a nervous breakdown. Ever since then everybody had treated Mark's dad as though he were crazy. His dad lost his job and couldn't find another. Even relatives like Aunt Beryl stared at Mark's dad with funny looks on their faces, as if he had changed into someone they didn't recognize.

"Okay, okay," Bill said. "Don't get mad!"

"I'm sorry," Mark said more softly, "but I hate it when people are labeled like that. Just because the guy is different, you don't have to say he's retarded."

Later in the day, Mark saw Edward walking toward the school library. He caught up to him again and smiled. "Hi. You look lost. Can I help?"

Edward stood there for a moment as if he were trying to decide what to do. Then he shoved a slip of paper at Mark. On it was written the title of a book on English grammar.

They went into the library together. Edward was much taller than Mark. He was well over six feet tall. Mark figured Edward might make a good addition to their basketball team.

Mark could feel kids staring at him as he walked with Edward. Even the librarian seemed uneasy as she gave Edward his library card. She looked at Edward as if he were sick or something.

Mark felt angry again. He kept thinking about how people treated his dad.

As they left the library, Mark glanced at Edward and smiled again. "Well, you're all set, Ed."

Edward was breathing hard. He was shifting his weight from one foot to the other, and Mark could see perspiration running down his face. He seemed to want to tell Mark something. Finally he made a sound. Mark smiled, figuring that was Ed's way of saying thank you.

Mark grinned widely. "Glad to help. See you in class, Ed."

After the last bell of the day, Mark and Grace and a dozen other students who lived west of the school waited for the bus. A girl said to Mark, "I saw you walking with that new guy. Man, he scares me. He just watches everybody. And he's real big. He reminds me of King Kong."

"He's nice. Just a little shy," Mark said.

"Gives me the creeps just the same," the girl replied with a shiver.

Mark tightened his lips angrily. He guessed that his dad gave people the creeps, too. That was why nobody would hire him after he had the nervous breakdown. It hurt Mark to see his dad go out for job interviews and come home empty-handed. It seemed that with every passing day, his father's shoulders slumped a little more. His father had once been a handsome man. Now he seemed almost as old as old Mr. Velliers.

Mark and Grace sat together on the bus ride home. Mark slumped down in the seat and mumbled, "Sometimes I hate Marnard. I'd like to go to a place like

New York. Nobody knows anybody in New York. You can sort of get lost in the crowd."

Grace nodded. "Yeah. Small towns can be a pain all right. Everybody knows everybody else's business."

Hugh Velliers was sitting behind Mark and Grace. He leaned forward. "Hey, Mark, my grandfather is really upset."

Mark turned around. "Yeah? Why?" Hugh was one month older than Mark. They had grown up together and were pretty good friends.

"The cornfield. It's really weird. Looks like nothing is going to grow there again," Hugh said.

"Well, it *was* burned in the fire," Grace said.

"But that shouldn't damage the soil," Mark said. "In fact, burning a field is supposed to be good for the soil."

"My grandfather wants to sue somebody," Hugh said.

Grace laughed. "Who's he going to sue? Little green men from planets unknown?"

"Aw, come on, Grace." Hugh frowned.

"My grandfather thinks those people who came to investigate know what happened and just won't talk. He says he should be paid for his ruined land."

"Probably lightning struck the field, that's all," Mark said. He really didn't believe that, but he didn't know what else to believe.

"Something real strange is happening around here," Hugh said. He sounded like his grandfather. "I don't know exactly what, but all those storms and now— Well, don't laugh, but that new guy, that Edward Thomas, he seems—I'm not sure, but he seems like the storms. You know, sort of unnatural."

"Oh, Hugh. Not you, too. What's the matter with you?" Mark snapped. His voice was so loud that everybody in the bus turned and looked at him. Mark knew he had to calm down. But honestly, he thought, people are too quick to label someone just because that person is different.

Somebody in the back of the bus whispered, "He gets mad real fast. His dad, you know: c-r-a-z-y."

Mark felt his heart pound in rage. He wished the bus would get to his farmhouse fast. He wanted to get away from all these narrow-minded people and their stupid talk. He wanted to take off his shoes and socks and go to the little stream behind his house. It was about the only pretty place around Marnard. Beside the stream, in the black and soggy ground, stood big trees. When Mark walked barefoot on the ground, he felt good all over.

Mark could still hear Hugh talking to the boy beside him about the cornfield. The other boy suddenly said, "Hey, know what? Maybe that weird Thomas guy is an alien."

There was an explosion of laughter, and Mark began to shiver. He felt ice-cold. It was as though a blast of midwinter air had just whipped through the bus.

2 WHEN THE BUS stopped, Mark hurried toward the stream. His father was already there. His shoulders seemed more slumped than usual. Mark could tell that his father was feeling low again.

"Hi, Dad," Mark called, trying to be cheerful.

His father turned and tried to smile. He looked so tired. "Hi, Mark."

Mark took off his shoes and socks and sank his feet into the cool stream. "Hot today, huh, Dad?"

"I guess so." His father's eyes were sad and blank.

"Dad—were you helping Mr. Conley build his barn today?" The only work Mark's father got now was odd jobs from neighbors. They gave him work—out of pity sometimes. Their pity seemed to hurt his father most of all.

"Yeah. It'll be done tomorrow. Then I think I'll go over to Springville and put my application in at the new insurance agency." Before his illness, Mark's dad had worked in insurance. "If I get the job, it'll mean moving from Marnard."

Mark had never lived anywhere else in his life. He was born in a little white farmhouse with a big porch. "That'd be okay, Dad."

His father picked up a stone and hurled it into the stream. "I would hate to leave myself," he said. "But a job is a job."

Mark chewed his lower lip. It was a nervous habit he'd just gotten into in the last year. He couldn't recall exactly, but it seemed he'd started it following the day he'd seen his father cry. He'd never seen his father cry before. It had been a terrible experience.

Mark's dad had once been a helicopter pilot for the police. He'd flown on mercy missions between Springville and Marnard. He'd also been the best insurance man in the county.

Mark had always thought his dad was tough as nails. But when they fired him from his insurance job, he had cried. And Mark had never forgotten that sight.

A wind came up. "Might rain, huh, Dad?"

"Just might at that. We could use it around here."

"Dad—listen, don't worry so much, okay?" Mark begged.

His father tried to smile. "I won't, son."

Just then Mark spotted old Velliers and Hugh approaching them. "Hello, Steve," Mr. Velliers called to Mark's dad. "You got any ideas on how to grow crops on cursed ground?"

"Cursed?" Mark's dad asked.

"Yeah, something's wrong," Hugh said. He looked at Mark. "Did you tell your dad about that strange new guy at school?"

Mark shrugged. "Edward Thomas. He's okay."

"He can't talk," Hugh added, "and some of the kids are scared of him."

"He's okay. He's just shy," Mark snapped. He quickly got up and hurried to the house, ashamed that his temper had flared again.

At dinner that evening, Mark's mother said she planned to work more overtime at the grocery store in Marnard. Mark noticed that his father's shoulders slumped even lower when she said that. His father must see the decision as another sign of his own failure, Mark realized.

"The opportunity just came up," Mark's mother said quickly. "It would be nice to have the extra responsibility. It could even lead to a manager's job."

Mark exchanged a look with Grace. They knew their mother really didn't enjoy the grocery store job. In fact, she'd talked about quitting and looking for another job. Now here she was talking about putting in *more* time at the store.

To change the subject, Grace mentioned the new boy at school. Her mother smiled. "Well, if there are new people in town, we ought to welcome them properly. We could bake a nice cake and take it to them."

"That would be great," Mark said.

"You find out where they live, and we'll take a cake to them on Saturday."

That night Mark lay awake, watching

the moon rise. He thought about his father and how miserable he had looked at dinner. He thought about Edward Thomas and how lousy everybody was acting toward him. "People are rotten!" Mark angrily muttered to himself.

Later on, a slashing rain struck the windows and Mark got up. Zigzag lightning cut through the sky. The thunder growled like a wild beast.

Mark went into the kitchen and was surprised to find his mother up, too. "Couldn't you sleep either, Mom?"

"I guess not. Those howling dogs!"

"Dogs?" Mark went to the door and opened it a little. Now he heard them, too. Mr. Velliers had his hounds out! "He can't be hunting on a night like this—"

Sheets of silver rain danced in the darkness. The sounds of the dogs grew louder. Suddenly Mark saw men in shiny black raincoats coming out of the shadows. "It's Hugh's father and grandfather, Mom."

When they got to the door, old Mr. Velliers shouted, "Hugh's disappeared!

Is Steve up?"

At that moment, both Grace and her father came into the kitchen. Mr. Velliers continued, "Was along about midnight I heard this ruckus outside. The dogs were going crazy. Hugh got up to check what it was. He didn't come back. Then my son and I went out. Couldn't find Hugh nowhere."

Hugh's father, a tall, grim-looking man, spoke harshly. "I'm afraid something's happened to my son."

"Mark and I will help you search," Mark's father said.

"And I'll call the sheriff and neighbors," Mark's mother added.

Mark's dad got into his rain gear and Mark did the same. Then they followed the Velliers out into the driving rain.

Soon the rain began to slacken. About five minutes later, it stopped entirely. But the land was covered with broad, muddy pools of water.

"You sure you looked everywhere at your place?" Mark asked Mr. Velliers.

"Everyplace," the old man said.

Nevertheless, Mark and his father decided to look again. They went to the Velliers' barn and poked around the corners.

"Hey, look!" Mark shouted. He pointed to a chicken with its head torn off.

Mark's dad shook his head. "It'd take a powerful human being to do that."

"Here's another one, Dad," Mark said softly.

Just then they heard a groan coming from a pile of hay. They both hurried towards the sound and found a body.

"We found Hugh!" Mark's dad shouted, bringing old Velliers and his son on the run.

Hugh looked wet, muddy, and drained, but his eyes were open. Everybody crowded around him. To their anxious questions, he mumbled, "I'm okay."

"What happened, boy?" his father asked him.

"I—I found the chickens. Then somebody came up behind me—got an arm around my throat. I just couldn't breathe. I thought I was being killed— like the chickens. I guess I passed out."

"Ought to get a doctor to look at you," Mark's dad said.

"Not tonight," Hugh said. "I'm okay. I just want to go to bed."

Old Velliers muttered, "Could have broke your neck. What kind of people are poking 'round out here in the night? Tearing off the heads of chickens. Nearly killing somebody on his own property."

"He had big strong hands," Hugh said. "He was more like some kind of animal than a person—"

Mark instantly thought of Edward Thomas and his huge hands. He remembered what the girl had said: *he reminds me of King Kong!* He hoped no one else would remember and was angry with himself for even thinking Edward Thomas was in any way connected with what had just happened.

"Must have been a crazy person," old Velliers said.

"Or maybe a hungry person," Mark's dad said softly.

"Hungry men don't rip the heads off chickens and almost kill a boy!" Velliers snapped.

The Scotts went home then. There wasn't much left of the night. Dawn came clear and bright within an hour.

"Did you really see the chickens?" Grace asked Mark as they waited for the bus.

"Yeah."

"Man, he must have been a powerful guy," Grace said.

"I guess."

"Remember the Marvin kids stealing all those chickens?" Grace said. "They were hungry all the time, those kids. Olie used to steal from everybody's lunch boxes at school, too."

Mr. Marvin had run off and left a wife and three children. Everybody heard about it. Then last year Mrs. Marvin moved away. Nobody in town ever knew where she had gone.

In class that day, Edward Thomas had a tape recorder with him. He was recording the lecture. Mark figured someone in his family would listen to the tape and tell him what the teacher had said.

When Mark entered the classroom, Edward turned and seemed to smile. Mark grinned back. Mark still felt guilty for imagining that Edward might have been the person who had killed the chickens and attacked Hugh. The person who really did those things was probably some drifter. And by now he would be in another county.

At lunchtime Mark tried to ask Edward for his address. However, Edward didn't seem to understand what Mark wanted.

After lunch Mark went to the school office. "My family would like to take a kind of welcome-to-town gift to the Thomas family. I'd like Edward's address."

Ms. Brent, the office manager, smiled. "What a nice idea. We always used to do that in the old days. Bless you folks for sticking with such a warm custom." She flipped through her files. "Oh, yes. Edward lives at the old Marvin place."

"Thanks, Ms. Brent," Mark said.

Mark was puzzled. The Marvin place had burned down in one of the lightning storms. Mark remembered seeing the scorched chimney looking like a black finger pointing at the sky. Even the foundation stones were blackened. There was nothing left but a run-down barn.

After school, Mark saw Edward get on a bike and head north. The Marvin place was about two and a half miles out. Yet the way Edward unsteadily pumped the bike, it might as well have been twice the distance. He almost fell off the bike twice. Mark wondered why a boy his age had so much trouble riding a bike.

"Hey," Grace exclaimed as she came up, "isn't that Olie Marvin's old orange bike?"

"Yeah, that's right," Mark said. He remembered the Christmas Olie had gotten the bike. It was secondhand and rusted, so Mrs. Marvin had painted it orange to cover the rust marks. "Edward lives at the old Marvin place now."

"But the house burned down," Grace said.

"I guess they must have made the barn into a house."

Grace shook her head. "That barn wasn't fit for animals."

"I guess they're making their way somehow," Mark replied.

Saturday dawned cloudy and cooler. The blue sky was tinged with rippled clouds. Grace and Mark—under their mother's directions—had baked a beautiful strawberry cake with thick strawberry frosting. In green icing it read, "Welcome to Marnard."

After the pickup truck was in motion, Mark's mother said, "I wonder what they've done with the Marvin place."

Mark shook his head. He was afraid of what they would find. Even the trees in front of the farmhouse had been burned. "Mom, don't be surprised if the Thomas family is sort of—well, different. I think they might be from the hills. I mean, Edward can't even ride a bike well."

His mother smiled. "I understand. I'm not quick to judge people just because they're different."

They left the asphalt highway and turned onto a dirt road.

"There's the Marvin place," Grace said, "and everything still looks horrible from the fire."

Mark looked around. A big old oak tree stood in front of the property. The lightning had divided the tree's massive trunk. The branches hung down lifeless.

"This place scares me," Grace said when they stopped.

Mark remembered the farm as it had been when Mr. Marvin lived there. Poor Mr. Marvin—skinny, hunched-over shoulders, a red peeling nose. It seemed as if the farm were still haunted by his sad spirit.

Mark's mother lifted the strawberry cake out of the pickup truck. The pretty cake seemed almost ridiculous in this charred place with its dying trees.

"They must be living in the barn," Mark said.

The three walked toward the barn, crossing the broken foundation stones of the house.

Suddenly they heard a savage hiss. Mark turned sharply to see the thick body of an angry snake moving underneath a chunk of broken pottery.

"Look out!" Mark screamed at his mother and sister.

3 MRS. SCOTT AND Grace jumped away from the angry snake. Mark saw then that it was only a bull snake, not a rattler.

"Wow, he's big!" Grace exclaimed.

The snake made the place seem more depressing. Only a few years ago, the farm had been alive with the shouts of the Marvin kids. Now a snake lived in the foundation stones.

They walked on to the barn and stopped. It was broken down and looked like a beached ship. There were holes in the walls and only a few scaly shreds of paint hung on the boards.

"Maybe we shouldn't have come," Mark said.

His mother turned to him. "Well, we did. And we're going to finish what we came to do," she declared.

"Hello! Anybody home?" Mark shouted. There was no answer. He rapped on the big double doors. Slowly one of the doors opened a crack. A young man stood inside. He was taller than Edward and had the same blue eyes.

"Hi," Mark said, "we're the Scotts. I go to school with Edward. We just wanted to welcome you to Marnard."

Mark's mother held out the cake. "This is for you and your family."

The man stared at the cake as if he had never seen anything like it before. His clothes were as ill-fitting as the ones Edward had worn. Suddenly Mark realized that the old clothes were some that the Marvins had left behind.

"We live about four miles from here," Mark's mother said. "If there's ever anything we can do for you, just come and ask. Our house is the one with the big green mailbox. You can't miss it."

The strange man finally took the cake. He looked down at it and made a sound. It was not really speech, just a sound. He pointed to his mouth and ears and he shook his head.

"Oh, I understand. You can't hear." Mark's mother smiled, and then spoke more clearly. "We just wanted to welcome you to Marnard with the cake."

He nodded. Then he closed the door.

The Scotts looked at one another. There seemed nothing else to do but go home.

"Maybe it's just the two guys on their own," Mark said as they started back.

"I bet they're runaways," Grace said.

"Grace, be sensible. We don't know anything of the kind," Mrs. Scott said.

"Both of them are deaf," Mark said, "and they look alike. Must be brothers."

"I hope they don't think we came just to be nosy," Mark's mother worried.

"If they did run away from someplace, I bet they don't want visitors," Grace said. She glanced back at the barn. "I just saw the burlap on the window move. I think they were watching us."

"They sure must be poor to live like that," Mark said.

"Well, being poor is no disgrace," his mother commented.

Grace leaned back on the seat, her hair flying in the wind. "I'm going to be rich when I get older," she said firmly.

"You don't have to be rich to be happy," her mother replied. She meant what she said. Yet Mark couldn't help thinking she was referring to her own family as well as to the Thomas boys.

"Yeah," Grace said, "but I think it's easier to be happy when you're rich."

As they drove into the yard, Mark noticed his father standing out under the trees.

"He looks down, doesn't he?" Mark said.

"I bet he heard about that job in Springville," Grace said, swinging open the door.

"Don't ask him about it, okay?" Mrs. Scott whispered.

The three of them started telling all about the Thomas family. Mark's dad listened and nodded, but his mind seemed to be somewhere else.

Finally he said, "I hope none of you had your heart set on moving to Springville."

"I like it fine right here," Mark said quickly.

"Me, too," Grace said. "I'd hate to leave my friends."

"Well, that's good because I didn't get the job. They said I was well qualified, but they hired somebody else." He stuck his hands in his pockets and turned away from his family. "They hired someone who isn't crazy."

"Oh, Steve!" Mark's mother cried.

Mark's father turned away and walked toward the stream behind the house. After a moment's hesitation, Mark followed him.

The two walked together in silence for a time. Then Mark quietly asked, "Dad, where does the stream empty?"

"The Platte," he said as he kicked a clod of earth. "You know, Mark, I sometimes wonder why my grandfather settled here. Bleak land, when you come to think of it."

"Yeah, but it gets to you after a while," Mark said.

"Mark, did you ever read any Stephen Vincent Benet in your English classes?"

"Yeah, a little."

"He was a favorite of mine when I was a boy. I remember one line he wrote: 'I died in my boots like a pioneer . . . with the whole wide sky above me.' I thought that was beautiful."

"Yeah, Dad. It is nice."

But Mark's mind wasn't on the poem. Instead he was worrying about his father. He looked awfully depressed.

Mark searched his memory for something to cheer his father. He brightened with a sudden idea. "Hey, know what, Dad? We ought to canoe down the river this summer like we did a few years back. Remember?"

"We don't have a canoe."

"Hugh Velliers does. He'd loan it to me, Dad."

"Well, maybe. We'll see." He turned then and walked back toward the house.

Mark stood by the stream awhile longer. He was watching tadpoles in the clear water when a girl's voice startled him. "Hi, Mark. How's the water?"

Mark turned. "Jeannie? Jeannie Bryant?" he asked in disbelief. He hadn't seen Jeannie in years! Yet here she stood—and looking more beautiful than ever. With her high cheekbones and willowy figure, she looked like a New York model.

"Yeah. You look like you're not sure. Have I changed that much in two years?" She laughed.

When Mark was in junior high, he had dated Jeannie. Then her family had moved away.

"You look terrific, Jeannie. Hey, are you here for a visit?"

"I'm staying with Bill." Jeannie and Bill were cousins. "I'll be going to school with you and everything. I'll be here all summer, too." She pushed her long, dark, wavy hair from her face and grinned. "Oh, by the way, Mark, you look terrific, too."

Mark dropped his eyes, a little embarrassed. Jeannie stared at him for a moment as she nibbled a stalk of grass. Then she spun around and said over her shoulder, "See you, Mark." She was gone as quickly as a sunset.

Mark grinned in spite of himself. All of a sudden, the last weeks of school looked a lot more interesting.

He had really liked Jeannie when they used to date. The Bryants were the richest family in Marnard, but Jeannie never seemed stuck-up about it. Even when she was small and she had the only Shetland pony in town, she didn't brag or parade around.

Mark grinned down into the water. She'd said he looked *terrific*. His grin widened.

Just then Mark heard a gunshot. His smile vanished and he looked around quickly. It was somebody shooting at a brush rabbit, he told himself. But his heart was pounding with a secret fear. He ran toward the house, taking the steps two at a time.

"Dad?" Mark shouted.

His mother's voice answered from the kitchen. "Your father went for a walk."

Mark went into the den and checked the cupboard where his father kept his rifle and two pistols. One of the pistols was missing. Mark felt his legs grow weak. He prayed that his father had taken one of the pistols to show to

Mr. Velliers. That he hadn't taken it to—

Mark dashed outside and raced toward the Velliers' place. He found Hugh and his grandfather out working in the field.

"Has my dad been over here?" Mark asked breathlessly.

Old Velliers shook his head. "Haven't seen him."

"You sure?" Mark asked desperately.

"I got eyes, haven't I?" old Velliers muttered.

Mark looked at Hugh. "Did you just hear a shot?"

"Yeah," Hugh said. He saw the fear in Mark's eyes. "Yeah, I did hear a shot. I figured it was a hunter."

"Lot of them fools running around the woods," old Velliers said.

Hugh wiped the dirt off his hands. "Grandpa, Mark and I are going to check out that shot."

"Just a waste of time," the old man said.

"I'll be back real quick," Hugh promised.

"See that you are. Lot of work here."

Mark and Hugh ran into the field behind the farm. It was a scraggly looking place, overgrown with brush and a few trees.

Mark searched the darkening horizon. The sun was going down and the bobwhites were already calling to each other.

"It sounded like it came from around here," Mark said.

"Yeah. But sometimes you can't really tell the direction of a sound," Hugh said.

Mark figured that Hugh had probably guessed what his fears were.

"Mark," Hugh said, "is your dad out hunting maybe?"

"I don't know. His pistol is missing—but not the rifle. I mean, if he were hunting—" Mark felt sick to his stomach.

Hugh looked at Mark. "Your dad has been real worried lately, hasn't he? I mean about not getting a job."

"Yeah. He went out for a job in Springville and they turned him down. He found out today—"

Hugh nodded. He knew what Mark's

fears were, all right. But he didn't say anything except, "Let's keep looking."

Mark remembered the look on his father's face when he recited the Benet lines: *I died in my boots like a pioneer . . . with the whole wide sky above me.*

Mark's heart pounded harder and louder. But it wasn't loud enough to drown out his own desperate fears.

4 THE SHADOWS WERE falling from the trees as the boys came to a clearing. Suddenly another shot rang out. It was close, so close that Mark could smell the gunpowder.

In a moment, a giant of a man came running through the brush. He carried two dead rabbits. He didn't stop when he saw the boys. He just kept right on running.

"Who was that?" Hugh exclaimed. "I've never seen him before."

"Edward Thomas' brother. I saw him today. I guess he must have been the one shooting." Mark gave a sigh of relief. Then he clapped Hugh on the back and smiled. "Hey, Hugh, thanks for coming with me."

Hugh grinned. "You bet. See you later."

Mark hurried home. When he got to the front porch, he could smell the beef stew. He rushed up the steps. He knew he was late for dinner. They were probably waiting for him.

"Mark, where on earth have you been?"

his mother asked.

"I was just messing around," Mark said.

Mark's father looked up from the table. "I hope you weren't bird-dogging me."

" 'Course not, Dad," Mark lied.

"I took a long walk," his father said. "Just wanted to be alone and to do some thinking."

"I heard some shooting out there," Grace commented as she dished out the peas.

Mark's father glanced at his son. "Did you think I was shooting myself or something? Is that why you were out there?"

"Aw, Dad!" Mark said, but he couldn't look his father in the eye. He wasn't very good at lying.

"Great. Now even my own family thinks I'm crazy!"

"Steve, please!" Mark's mother begged.

Mark had never seen both his parents so much on edge. It made him feel uncomfortable and sick.

Suddenly his father got up and angrily shoved his chair underneath the table. It made a horrible grating sound. Then he stomped outside, slamming the door behind him.

The rest of the family sat in painful silence. Finally Mark spoke. "I'm sorry if I caused trouble, Mom."

"You didn't. I don't blame you for worrying when you heard the shot. Your father has been depressed lately. Nobody will give him a chance. He even called Henry Baldwin—he begged Mr. Baldwin to give him his old job back at the agency."

Mark had known Mr. Baldwin for as long as he could remember. Mr. Baldwin was a jolly, heavy-set man. Mark had always liked him—up until the time he wouldn't let Mark's dad come back to work because of his illness. Mr. Baldwin even admitted that Steve Scott was the best insurance agent he had ever had. But he said it would make the customers "nervous" to deal with a man who had a history of mental illness.

Mark's mother continued in a sad voice, "Mr. Baldwin was very nice. He claimed *he* wanted your father back. But he said other people might be uncomfortable. Your poor father. He felt so bad he almost cried."

"How can people be so stupid?" Mark said bitterly.

They let the ugly subject die. But the meal was spoiled, and everyone in the house was uneasy for the rest of the night.

Mark was glad to go to school Monday just to escape the house. A pleasant surprise in chemistry class helped him feel a little better. As he entered the room, Edward Thomas stood up and walked over to him. He pressed a note into Mark's hand. Mark opened and read the carefully printed message:

thenk u for stawbary kake.

It was signed Edward and Jules Thomas.

Mark smiled and Edward smiled back.

Then Edward shyly returned to his seat.

Just before the bell rang, Jeannie Bryant came into class. She quickly took the seat next to Mark's. She gave him a warm smile and immediately said, "Mark, I've got a personal question for you. Who are you going with to the prom? Is it somebody I know?"

Mark shrugged. "I sort of didn't plan on going. I'm not going with anybody, and I don't dance very well."

"Oh, that would be a shame," Jeannie said, putting on a sad face. "But maybe that means you could help me out. See, nobody remembers me, Mark, and I'm afraid I won't get anybody to go with me. And I just love dancing." She smoothed back her hair and arched her neck. She knew how to use her looks, that was for sure.

Mark realized what she was asking. Nervously he said, "Uh—I'd sure like to go with you, Jeannie."

"Would you, Mark?" she exclaimed in delight.

Mark felt as though everybody in the

room was looking at him. "Yeah, I would," he said.

"That's terrific," Jeannie said. "Oh, we'll really have a great time! I can hardly wait!"

Mark didn't hear much of the chemistry lecture after that. Jeannie Bryant was such a pretty girl. When she attended school here before, she had been the most popular girl in class. Mark couldn't understand how she could ever be hard up for a date. None of the other guys could have forgotten her.

After chemistry, Hugh Velliers fell in step beside Mark. "I just heard a rumor about you, Mark."

"Yeah? What's that?"

"You and Jeannie Bryant are going to the prom together," Hugh said.

Mark nodded. "I guess so."

"Man, how did you work that out? I called her the first night she got into Marnard and she gave me the cold shoulder. Some of the other guys asked her, too. She turned everybody down."

Mark remembered Jeannie's words:

*nobody remembers me, Mark, and I'm
afraid I won't get anybody to go with me.*
He was surprised that she had lied about
it. But he was still happy that *he* was going with her to the prom.

At lunch the news had reached Grace,
and she hurried over to tease Mark.
"Hey, Romeo," she giggled, "where's
Juliet?"

"Knock it off, Grace," Mark said.
"Jeannie and I are just old friends."

"Maybe so. But even the junior high
girls think you're cute, Mark Joseph
Scott," Grace laughed.

"Come on," Mark groaned.

"Okay," Grace smiled, "but it's true.
Even if you are my brother, you're still
the best-looking guy in school. That's the
real reason Jeannie Bryant is going with
you.

"Remember how Jeannie always
wanted the best of everything? Mom said
Jeannie looked at fifty Shetland ponies
before she found one she liked. And
remember they had to send away for all
her clothes? She always said there wasn't

anything good enough in Marnard."

Mark had forgotten all that. He just remembered Jeannie as a nice, pretty girl. Yet now that he thought about it, it made him feel weird to think she'd probably looked over all the guys like she'd looked over those ponies. But then there was some honor in being picked as the best, wasn't there?

Mark always ate lunch quickly to make time for some basketball practice. That's what he was doing when Jeannie found him. As he sunk a hook shot, she smiled admiringly. "You were always a good athlete," she commented.

"I'm fair," Mark said.

"Bet you win the championship for the school."

"Naw, not me. We got a new kid here, though. He's really tall. He might turn out to be a good player. I'm going to try to get him on the team next year. His name is Edward Thomas."

Jeannie made a face. "Oh, him! I wouldn't be too eager to get him on the team if I were you, Mark. He's ugly and he seems retarded. He can't even talk."

Mark hated to hear Jeannie say something so cruel. "He *isn't* ugly, Jeannie. He just takes a little getting used to. And he got a C on the last chemistry test, which is pretty good."

Jeannie gave a sharp laugh. "Well then, he must be cheating. Anyway, all the kids say he's weird."

"Jeannie," Mark said sharply, "Ed isn't weird and he doesn't cheat. You can't cheat in chemistry class. Ms. Armstrong marches around like a drill sergeant watching everybody."

"Okay, okay, Mark. But you've got to admit he *is* a little strange."

"Just because he's deaf and new at school doesn't make him strange. I wish everybody would just be nice to the poor guy. That's why I think getting him on the basketball team might help. People could see that Ed's okay, and Ed could get to meet new people."

Jeannie frowned. "Listen, Mark, I'm not sure the other guys would want Ed on the team. I mean, he looks like a gorilla. I heard that he lifted an engine off the block in shop the other day. Do you know what some of the kids are saying? They think he was the one who ripped the heads off those chickens and almost killed Hugh Velliers."

"Nobody has any reason to say that," Mark said.

Jeannie shrugged. "Well, let's not talk about him. It's obvious we don't agree." She smiled and laid her hand on Mark's shoulder.

"Anyway," she added, "whoever was responsible, I guess Hugh is lucky he wasn't killed the other night."

"I don't think Hugh is so lucky," Mark said. "He couldn't get you to go to the prom with him."

Jeannie blinked. Then she smiled. "Oh. You found out, huh? Well, I didn't want to go with him, that's all. He's nice and all that, but I like you better."

Mark stared at her. "Why, Jeannie?"

"Oh, Mark. It's just a lot of things. We were always good friends when I lived here before, weren't we? Anyway—" She did a little pirouette, and Mark remembered she'd been the only child in town who took dancing lessons in Springville. Her parents drove her seventy-five miles round trip each week for those lessons. "Anyway, Mark, you're the best catch at Marnard High."

Mark frowned. "The best 'catch'?"

"Sure. Why shouldn't I be honest? We were always honest with each other, weren't we, Mark? Isn't that one of the things you said you liked about me?

"See, the other night I got together with a couple of my old friends and we went through last year's annual. We looked at pictures of all the boys. I remembered most of the boys, but everybody has changed so much. Jeff used to be handsome, but now he's got that awful skin. And Harry turned out to be so fat.

"We looked at all the pictures and rated the guys. You know, ten points for perfect and one point for just being alive and breathing. Well, you got a nine, Mark."

"Like at a dog show, huh, Jeannie?"

Mark said without smiling. "Best of the breed."

Jeannie laughed and gave Mark a playful shove. "Oh, come on. Where's your sense of humor? Don't tell me the guys don't rate the girls. Maybe you don't give points, but everybody knows who's worth dating."

Mark tried to be good-humored about it. He smiled a little and went back to his basketball. Then the bell rang for afternoon classes, and he hurried to his next class.

When Mark took his seat in English later that afternoon, Hugh looked up. "Well, if it isn't God's gift to women."

"What's that supposed to mean?" Mark snapped. Hugh surprised him by being such a poor loser. Mark had always liked Hugh, and he expected more class from his friend. But then he wondered, how would he feel if the tables were turned? Maybe he'd be a poor loser, too.

"Never mind," Hugh grunted.

Mark stared at his friend. Hugh really didn't look too good—like he was coming down with the flu or something. Mark figured Hugh probably had a headache that was making him bad-tempered.

Ms. Krause wasn't in class that day. Instead, a very old, white-haired lady took her place.

"Good afternoon, class," she said. "I'll be your substitute teacher today. Some of you may know me. I am Mrs. Gunther. I used to teach here years ago. In fact, I taught many of your parents."

Bill leaned over to Mark. "She must be eighty years old! My mom had her in English, and Gunther was in her fifties then. Mom said the kids used to call her 'the wicked witch of the west.' "

"You've been assigned to read *The Great Gatsby,* is that right, children?" Mrs. Gunther asked.

At the word "children," Bill Bryant roared with laughter. Mrs. Gunther glared at him. "Either share your joke, young man, or keep silent," she warned. Then she asked her question again.

"Yeah, that's right," a girl said.

"Very well," Mrs. Gunther said. "Then

that's what we'll be discussing today. Fitzgerald is a very interesting writer. Though to my mind, not all that inspiring. I prefer books with a real message. For instance, Hawthorne's works. Have any of you ever read one of Nathaniel Hawthorne's stories?''

No hands went up.

"That's a shame. I think today's children really need books that will build character and values.''

Bill snickered again. He turned and whispered to the girl next to him, "Man, they really scraped the bottom of the barrel to dig up this old bat.''

"Shhh!" Mark said. But it was too late; Mrs. Gunther had very good hearing. She looked right at Bill. "What is your name, young man?''

"Uh—you mean me?" Bill asked nervously. He was the captain of the basketball team. He knew if a teacher had any trouble with him, he could get thrown off the team. The team was the most important thing in his life.

"Yes, you," Mrs. Gunther said.

"I'm Bill Bryant," he said.

"I believe you were trying to insult me, Mr. Bryant."

"No, ma'am," Bill lied. "I wasn't saying anything insulting. You must have misunderstood me."

"First insults and now lies," Mrs. Gunther said. "Very well. While the rest of the class is discussing the assignment, you will come to the board and write one hundred times, 'I will not be rude.'" Mark guessed that was the way her generation of teachers disciplined students.

Bill frowned angrily.

"Mrs. Gunther," a boy said, "our regular teachers don't make us write stuff like that. We just get marked down in citizenship."

"Thank you for the information," Mrs. Gunther said, "but I think this punishment suits the crime. So, Mr. Bryant, will you begin immediately?"

Bill looked like he was going to die. Half the kids in the class were choking back laughter.

Mark whispered to him, "Go on and do it. It's not that bad."

But Bill had a lot of pride. He knew he would never live down having to write on the board like a little kid. "Look," he almost shouted, "I didn't say what you think I said!"

Mrs. Gunther smiled sweetly. "It's fortunate this is the last class of the day. That means you won't miss any classes when you add another fifty sentences to the original one hundred."

Bill looked like he was going to explode. He finally got out of his chair and went to the board. As he wrote his first sentence, most of the class was in silent hysterics.

Yet Mark wasn't watching the class. He was staring at Bill's face. He had never seen such hate on anybody's face. Bill looked like he wanted to kill someone!

5 WHILE BILL WROTE his sentences, the class talked about the assignment. When the last bell rang, everybody left except Bill. He still had over fifty sentences to go.

Outside the classroom, a girl said, "I wonder what happened to Krause. She was fine this morning."

Another girl said, "I heard she collapsed in the middle of her Shakespeare class. Somebody said it was real sudden—a virus or something. There was a substitute in my PE class this afternoon, too. Must be something going around."

Hugh shook his head. "My head feels like an eggshell about to crack. Whatever is going around, I think I got it."

"Funny time of the year for a virus," Mark said.

Just then Edward Thomas came around the corner. He had a written assignment for Ms. Krause. When he saw the white-haired lady at the desk, he approached more slowly. He put the paper on her desk. Then he turned and looked at Bill. He'd obviously never seen anybody writing the same thing over and over on the board.

Bill felt his gaze and turned around. "What are you staring at?" he demanded. He might not have said it under better conditions, but he was so mad that he hated everybody. Frightened, Edward hurried away.

"Mr. Bryant," Mrs. Gunther cried.

"You saw him making fun of me!" Bill shouted.

"I saw no such thing. The boy was just looking at you. I think we'd better talk to the principal about your behavior!"

Ms. Armstrong, the chemistry teacher, was passing the room just as Bill shouted, "Look, I'll get kicked off the basketball team if I get in trouble with the principal!"

"You should have thought of that before," Mrs. Gunther said.

"Look, you old bat!" Bill shouted.

That was enough for Ms. Armstrong. She strode into the classroom and stared coldly at Bill. "Bill, don't you ever speak to a teacher that way! You'll report to the principal's office at once.''

Most of the students were still milling around outside the classroom when Bill, Ms. Armstrong, and Mrs. Gunther came out. Everyone had heard the angry voices coming from the room.

As Bill passed, Jeannie asked him, "What's going on, Bill?"

"That Thomas kid was bugging me and that—" Before Bill could finish, Ms. Armstrong stopped him. "Watch yourself, Bill. You're already in quite enough trouble."

Jeannie hurried after Ms. Armstrong. "What did Bill do?"

"Never mind," she said. Then she turned to the crowd of students. "Break it up, everybody. This isn't a circus!"

Nonetheless, a large group followed Bill to the principal's office. Mark and Jeannie tagged along, too.

As they stood outside the office, Grace arrived on the scene. "What's all the excitement about?" she asked.

"Bill's getting a bum rap," Jeannie said

bitterly. "And all because of something that Thomas guy did."

"No," Mark said, "I saw what happened. Bill was out of line. He insulted Mrs. Gunther. Then when he got in trouble, he tried to take it out on Ed Thomas."

"What is an old lady like that doing teaching anyway?" Jeannie said. "She looks like Mother Time or something."

"She's okay," Hugh said, still holding his head. "She really knows Fitzgerald. She taught us a lot."

Jeannie ignored him. "Poor Bill," she said. "I bet this gets him kicked off the team."

Inside the office, Bill desperately pleaded his case. But after listening to both sides, the principal told Bill he couldn't play basketball for the rest of the year.

"Please, Mr. Marston," Bill begged, "the team is depending on me. What about the championship?"

"Some things are more important than team standings," Mr. Marston replied.

"Treating teachers and other students with common decency, to name one."

Bill stumbled from the principal's office.

"What happened?" Jeannie asked him.

"The worst!" Bill groaned. "I'm off the team for the rest of the year."

"Tough break, Bill," Mark said. "But the year's almost over. You've got next year to think about."

"I don't care about next year!" Bill exploded. "The playoffs are coming up! Man, I'd like to punch that Edward Thomas in his stupid face! This is all his fault. If he hadn't come in just then and looked at me like I was some kind of idiot, I would have finished writing those dumb sentences and been home free! The jerk!"

Jeannie shook her head. "That guy Thomas shouldn't be in a regular school. I don't know why they don't send him to some special school for the retarded."

"Edward didn't mean any harm, Bill. You should have known that," Mark said.

Jeannie looked at Mark. "You don't understand how it is with types like

Thomas. They like to tease. It's how they get their kicks. There was one of them in a summer camp I went to. She used to tie everybody's clothes into knots just to drive us up the wall. The only peace we got was when we all got together and taught her a lesson."

"Edward isn't like that," Mark insisted. "He doesn't bother anybody. Why do you feel you have to put him down? If anyone around here is weird, it's you and your cousin. You got a wild imagination, both of you."

The more Mark talked to Jeannie, the less he liked her. Suddenly it wasn't so important anymore that she was beautiful.

Still, he wanted to make her see sense. "Jeannie," he said more softly, "it isn't fair to blame Edward because Bill got in trouble over a remark he made to a teacher."

Jeannie smiled. "Okay, Mark, maybe not. But I still feel sorry for Bill. Basketball is everything to him."

The buses came then and everybody

went in different directions.

At dinner that night Mark said, "A couple of teachers are down with a virus."

"Sam Velliers is very sick today, too," Mark's dad said. "He's so weak he can't get out of bed. He said it came on suddenly. Just cut his legs out from under him."

"Nobody seemed sick yesterday," Grace said, "but today a couple of kids in gym just felt terrible. Their parents had to come and take them home."

Mark's dad shook his head. "Sam is sure his sickness has something to do with the burned field."

"Yeah?" Grace looked interested. "How could that be, Dad?"

"Oh, he has this theory. He thinks that some kind of alien spaceship landed. According to him, the fire from the engines ruined his field. He thinks the ship took off again, but not before some deadly organisms escaped. He thinks that's what made him sick."

"What kind of organisms?" Grace asked, wide-eyed.

"Old Velliers says they could be anything," Mr. Scott said as he took another serving of beans.

"What does the doctor say?" Mark's mother asked.

"He came over, looked at Sam, and said he'd do some tests. He doesn't know what to make of it."

Following dinner, Mark and Grace went outside. Grace looked up at the stars. "Do you think there really are intelligent beings up there, Mark?" she asked.

"I'm not sure, Grace."

"It would be something, wouldn't it? I mean if some of them really came to earth. Man, that would be a big story, huh? It would have to be the most important story of the century. Maybe of all time!"

"I guess."

"Mark, know what? Edward Thomas isn't deaf."

Mark turned sharply to look at her. "Of course he is."

"Nope. Kid told me today that

somebody dropped a tool in shop and Edward turned and looked.''

"He probably felt it drop on the floor,'' Mark said.

"No, he heard it all right. Another thing, somebody saw him with earphones on, *listening* to that tape recorder of his. He's not deaf. He just pretends he is. I think he just doesn't speak English.''

"I don't believe that, Grace,'' Mark said. But he had to admit he was curious now. "I mean, if he spoke another language, why wouldn't he admit it? There isn't any disgrace in not being able to speak English.''

Grace leaned against the porch railing. "Maybe he speaks a language we never heard of before.''

"Like what? Martian or Plutonian?'' Mark said scornfully.

"Maybe,'' Grace said. "You can laugh if you want to, but anything is possible. Like—well, maybe it *was* a spaceship that landed in Mr. Velliers' cornfield.''

A firefly blazed in the darkness. "Look, Grace,'' Mark laughed, "there goes another spaceship!"

"Okay, wise guy," Grace said. "You can make fun of me all you want. But it could be true. Maybe those people out there are a lot like us. Maybe you could meet one right now and not know the difference. I mean, when rocks come from outer space—you know, meteorites—they look just like our rocks, don't they? So why couldn't people look the same, too?"

"You think Edward Thomas is an alien?" Mark demanded.

"No. I guess I really don't."

"Well, Grace, what do you mean then?"

She turned and looked hard at Mark. "I mean—he *could* be an alien, couldn't he? He came to Marnard right after the fire in the cornfield. He can't speak our language. He looks sort of different. He acts funny."

"Aw, Grace, go on in the house and do your homework!" Mark said.

"Okay, okay. I didn't say he *was* an alien. I just said he *could be*. That's all." Grace skipped across the porch and went inside.

Mark stayed outside a few minutes longer. As he watched the sky darken, he saw stars appear like sparks from a huge fire.

It was so crazy, he thought, to be wondering if Edward Thomas was an alien. But then so many crazy things had been happening in Marnard lately.

Mark remembered a science teacher he had had once. Mr. Melamid had said, "Only a fool believes in just that which he can see. Because what we see is often not even what really is. We should always be open to wonders and to truth. There are still so many wonders we haven't even dreamed of."

As he lay in bed that night, Mark wondered why such incredible things seemed more possible in the darkness. And still, was it so incredible? And what if others began to believe it?

It might be exciting for Grace to wonder if Edward Thomas was an alien. But the people in town would be terribly frightened. They might react like the people in Salem in the 1600s. Back in Salem, everything bad that happened was blamed on people who were said to be witches. As a result, innocent people were killed. The whole town went mad.

What if people began to believe Edward Thomas was causing the spread of some strange virus? Mark shuddered at the thought. Marnard could become another Salem.

6 ON THE SCHOOLBUS the next morning, Hugh was missing. He was by no means the only one; the bus was quite empty. It seemed the virus had spread. Even the regular driver had been replaced by a substitute.

When Mark arrived at school, he saw Bill Bryant going grimly to class with Jeannie. Mark caught up with them and said to Bill, "Listen, I know how bad you feel. But look at the bright side of it. School will be over for the year in no time. Next year you can make up the games you had to miss."

"She'll be sorry, that old bat," Bill said bitterly.

"Bill, talk like that is just going to get you into more trouble."

"Mind your own business," Bill snapped.

As Bill and his cousin moved off, Mark saw Bill had something hidden under his jacket. It looked like a large box. Curious, Mark watched them. Bill and Jeannie went outside under some trees. There they opened the box and Mark could see there was a sack inside. It was knotted at the top. After shaking the sack, Jeannie laughed and put the lid down. Then she waved goodbye to Bill and headed for chemistry.

Mark followed Jeannie and caught up with her. "What's in the box?" he asked.

Jeannie jumped a little. "Oh, Mark! Uh, just some fresh fruit for lunch."

"Oh."

"Well, see you later," she hurriedly said and gave him a strange smile.

Jeannie's odd behavior made Mark more curious. He watched as she turned and hurried to chemistry. Then he followed at a safe distance. Jeannie went into the classroom and Mark stood outside, looking in the window.

He saw Jeannie go up to Edward Thomas. She explained something to him using sign language. He finally seemed to understand. Then Jeannie handed the box to Edward and Edward got up. He hurried from the room and walked quickly down the hall—towards the English classroom. Jeannie had obviously sent

Edward on an errand.

Mark strongly suspected that Bill had a plot going and that Jeannie was helping him. Something about that box was supposed to get Edward in trouble and hurt Mrs. Gunther, too.

Mark hurried after Edward and caught him by the arm. "May I look in the box?" he asked Edward.

Edward seemed to understand him easily enough. He smiled and nodded.

Mark took the box and opened the lid. Then he loosened the rope on the sack and peered inside. A writhing, angry bull snake was inside!

Mark quickly closed and knotted the sack again.

"Were you taking this to Mrs. Gunther?" he asked.

Edward nodded. He hadn't seen what was in the sack.

"Did Jeannie tell you to do this?" Mark continued.

Edward nodded again.

"I'm going that way, Edward. I'll do it for you," Mark said.

Edward smiled and returned to chemistry.

Mark could see all too clearly what would have happened if he hadn't stopped Edward. Edward would have given the box to Mrs. Gunther, and she would have opened the sack. The poor woman might have been deeply frightened.

And Edward would be blamed. Everybody would think he was truly vicious, scaring an older teacher like that. He'd probably even get kicked out of school. That would mean Bill would get his revenge on both Mrs. Gunther and Edward.

Mark went to the biology lab. "I found this bull snake," he said. "Maybe you could add it to your natural history museum here."

The teacher was pleased. "Thanks Mark. That's a nice idea."

Mark then went on to his chemistry class.

All during class, he kept wondering if Jeannie knew exactly what was in the box. Maybe she thought it was just a practical joke. Maybe she never really looked in the sack.

Mark kept hoping Jeannie was only being used. He didn't want to believe that Jeannie would do something cruel on purpose.

At a break between classes, Mark decided to find out for sure. He located Jeannie at her locker.

"Hey, Jeannie, you know that box of fruit you had this morning? The one you gave Edward to deliver to Mrs. Gunther?"

Jeannie suddenly looked tense. "What about it?"

"Well, I delivered it. I was going to the school office anyway, so I saved Edward the trip. It was real nice of you and Bill to give Mrs. Gunther some fruit. I gave it to Ms. Brent in the office, and she said she'd put it in the faculty lounge. I bet the teachers are enjoying it right now."

Mark looked Jeannie right in the eye. "I told Ms. Brent it was a gift from you and your cousin. I said you wanted to show the teachers how much you appreciated them."

Jeannie gasped. "When did you give Brent the box?"

"Early this morning. Why? What's the problem?"

"You idiot!" Jeannie cried. "You've just ruined me—and Bill. We'll probably both be suspended from school!"

Mark didn't have to wonder anymore how much Jeannie knew about the trick. She knew everything. But Mark played dumb. "What are you talking about, Jeannie?"

"There was a snake in that sack! Bill wanted to get even with Gunther and Thomas. Now do you see what you've done! Oh, you idiot!" She glared at him in fury.

Mark stared at Jeannie. He had really liked her. She was the first girl he'd ever truly cared for. When she'd returned, he'd thought they could be good friends again. But that had been a dream.

It didn't really matter now how beautiful Jeannie was on the outside. There was so little beauty on the inside.

Mark said softly, "I figured out what you were trying to do. I took the sack from Edward and looked in it. When I saw the snake, I decided to take it to the biology lab."

"Oh, Mark, thank heavens!" Jeannie began to laugh with relief. "You really had me going there for a minute."

"Jeannie, why would you do such a terrible—such a stupid—thing? I can't believe you would have gotten involved," Mark said sadly.

"I know. I shouldn't have. It's just that Bill got such a lousy deal. I'm sorry I got mixed up in it."

Jeannie reached out and touched Mark's arm. "Hey, you're not all *that* mad at me, are you?"

"Let's just say I'm disappointed."

"I really am sorry. I never should have gotten mixed up in Bill's stupid idea. You've made mistakes, haven't you, Mark? I mean, you're not all that perfect, are you?" She smiled and said, "Forgive me, Mark?"

"Sure. But—uh, Jeannie, I don't think

either of us would have any fun if we went to the prom together. It's not that I'm so perfect or anything like that. I just don't feel right about us anymore. I think I'd probably spoil your fun if I took you. You'd be happier going with some other guy."

Jeannie's face twisted with anger. "You think you're better than me, don't you, Mark Scott? Well, let me tell you a few things. You're a stuck-up jerk. And I don't know what you have to be so stuck-up about either. Your family sure isn't much. You owe everybody in town, and your father can't get a job because he's—"

Jeannie stopped herself and bit her lip. Her eyes had grown wide with shock.

"Please, Jeannie," Mark whispered. "I'd like to remember something nice about you. Don't ruin it all."

Jeannie tried to say something but she choked on her words. She suddenly turned and dashed around the corner.

Mark slowly went on to his music class. Mr. Santelli usually taught music. He had a beautiful tenor voice and he had sung in Italy with La Scala. But today Mr. Marston, the principal, appeared in the classroom.

"I'm sorry to say Mr. Santelli is out with the virus," he explained. "You people will have to practice for the spring festival on your own. Who's the student director?"

"Hugh Velliers, but he's out sick, too," a boy said.

Mark looked around the room. More than half the students were gone.

"Well, then, go to the study hall and do your homework," Mr. Marston said wearily.

Mr. Marston didn't look so good himself, but maybe most of it was worry. Half his teachers were gone. Others were becoming ill.

As students packed up their books, one girl commented, "I never remember a sickness like this coming in the spring."

"I hope I don't get it," a boy added. "My sister's got it and she's really sick. She's never been so sick."

Classes that afternoon were strange. Most of them were not regular classes but study halls.

Rumors flew around the school. Somebody said that the disease control center in Atlanta was trying to find out what was causing the virus. Somebody else said that Marnard was the only place in the state where the virus had cropped up.

After school, Mark walked over to the Velliers' farm to see how Hugh was. Old Velliers met him at the screen door. "Stay away from the house, boy," the old man ordered. "We're all terrible sick!"

"I'm sorry, Mr. Velliers. Is Hugh any better?"

"He's worse, if anything. I tell you, boy, this whole thing ain't natural. We've never been this sick."

Mark said, "It's probably the flu. Just rest and take care of yourselves."

"It's not natural. It's like nothing we've seen before. It come with the fire in the cornfield. Whatever landed that night brought it."

"Mr. Velliers—" Mark began.

"I know, you think I'm touched in the head. Hugh thinks so, too. You young folks think you got all the answers, but you don't. I've been here seventy-seven years, and I never seen anything like a fire that takes the life from the soil. I never seen chickens with heads ripped off like that. It's not natural. None of it's natural, I tell you."

"There's got to be a simple explanation," Mark said.

"Could be they want us all to die, whoever *they* are. I got to get back to Hugh now." The old man shuffled off.

Mark stood there in the darkening day, chilled by his thoughts. It was happening. Fear was growing in Marnard. He had seen it in the faces of the students today. Even the teachers seemed afraid.

Mark had heard about how panic spreads. A lot of little frightening things happen. People begin to believe anything. Everything but the fear goes away. Common sense, kindness—it all goes. Nothing is left but the fear. Horrible, choking fear.

Half-believed words spoken in fun suddenly become terrible stepping stones to panic.

Mark remembered the first day on the bus, the boy's laughing voice: *Hey, know what? Maybe that weird Thomas guy is an alien.*

Everybody had laughed then. They were not laughing anymore. Their eyes were full of fear.

7 WHEN MARK REACHED his house, he heard his parents fighting. He hated it when they fought. He decided not to go inside. Instead, he sat down on the porch steps.

Then he saw Grace. She'd come out to escape the fighting, too.

"What is it about today?" Mark asked.

"The usual. Only worse," Grace said sadly.

"Poor Dad."

"He wants to go to Chicago and look for a job there." Grace picked up a stalk of grass.

"You mean just him alone?"

"Yeah. He said we should stay here and he'll send for us when he has a job. That's what made Mom mad. She said he just wants to run away. She said he wouldn't send for us at all. It would be like when Mr. Marvin left his family. He just never came back, and he didn't send any word either."

"Dad isn't like Mr. Marvin," Mark said. He thought about Mr. Marvin. He had always looked like a beaten scarecrow. But then Mark had only known him when he was having trouble. Maybe at one time in his life Mr. Marvin had stood proud and tall.

"I hope he doesn't go away," Grace said. She seemed close to tears. "I just know he wouldn't come back or send for us either. I just know it."

The sounds of fighting in the house had stopped. Mark slowly got up and went inside. He found his mother alone in the kitchen, making dinner.

Mark noticed her eyes were red. She's been crying, Mark realized, and that shocked him. His mother rarely cried.

Mark could tell she was angry. She beat the potatoes as though she were mad at them.

"Mom, where's Dad?" Mark quietly asked.

"He's outside. Thinking."

Mark paused. Then he asked, "He wants to go to Chicago, huh?"

His mother briskly nodded. "He thinks he can find a job there. He seems to think all his problems would just disappear in

Chicago.

"Well, I think he's only trying to run away from his problems," she continued. "And if he goes to Chicago, he'll end up living on the streets. His life will be finished—and part of ours, too. We'll never be a family again."

Mark's mother turned and looked at her son. "Oh, Mark, you don't know how he feels! He thinks he's worthless!"

Mark put an arm around her shoulder. "Try not to worry, Mom. I'll go talk to him."

Mark went outside and found his father by the stream behind the house. He was tossing little pebbles into the water.

Mark decided he would talk first about what was happening at school. Maybe that would get his father's mind off his own troubles.

"The virus has hit half the kids at school, Dad. Half the teachers, too. They're talking about closing the school if it doesn't get any better."

"Maybe they'll need me to substitute down there," Mark's father said bitterly.

"I have a degree in accounting. I could teach math."

Then he suddenly threw down his entire handful of pebbles in a rage. "But I don't think they'll ever get that desperate, do you? Nobody's desperate enough to want a crazy man for any kind of job."

"Please, Dad. Don't talk like that."

"It's true, Mark."

"Dad, if you go to Chicago, we *all* have to go. We're a family. We have to stick together."

Mark's dad turned. "If I went away, then your mother could apply for government aid. Mark, we just can't go on like this. *I* can't go on like this."

"It's got to be all of us together, Dad. There's no other way. We need you, Dad."

Mark's father turned again. His eyes were wet. "Do I really mean anything to you anymore? How can I when everybody else thinks I'm worth less than nothing!"

Mark found it hard to talk. He looked

down at the dirt at his feet. "Got to be all of us—together."

That ended the conversation for the night. The rest of the evening was spent in troubled silence.

On the following day, even more students were sick. When Mark was in the school office, he heard Ms. Brent on the phone. She seemed very upset. Mark listened for a minute.

"Mr. Velliers," she said in a shocked voice, "I'm sure that isn't true. Why, the Thomas boy isn't even ill. Well, of course, the principal will speak with you. Wait a minute and I'll ring his office."

She looked upset when she hung up.

"Mr. Velliers is blaming Edward Thomas for the virus, isn't he?" Mark said.

Ms. Brent looked up. "You know about it?"

"Yes. He told me the same thing."

"He actually believes that a—a spaceship landed in his cornfield and that the Thomas boy is an alien. And now the poor man thinks the boy is infecting everybody with the virus."

Ms. Brent shook her head. "I wonder if Mr. Velliers has a high fever and is delirious. I can't imagine what Mr. Marston will think about all this. But Mr. Velliers insisted on speaking with him. Heavens, it's all so wild."

On his way to chemistry, Mark ran into a boy from the basketball team.

"Hey, Mark, did you hear the news? Your neighbors—the Velliers—they think all this sickness is being spread by that guy Edward Thomas. The old man called my dad last night. My dad said I'd better keep away from Thomas just in case."

"You must be joking. That's crazy," Mark said.

Crazy or not, by the end of first period the school was buzzing with the story. Two students refused even to come to chemistry unless Edward Thomas was sent from the room. Ms. Armstrong had no choice but to send them to the principal's office.

Later that day Bill Bryant stopped Mark in the hall. "Well, it seems like that weirdo you like so much is the one who's making everybody sick."

"Bill, that's just a dumb rumor," Mark insisted.

"Yeah? Funny the virus came at the same time he did. You've heard of people being carriers of disease, haven't you? You don't even have to be sick, but you can sure give it to everybody else around you. That jerk ought to be kicked out of school."

There was no sense in trying to reason with Bill, Mark realized. Or Mr. Velliers. And how many others?

Mark wondered if Edward knew what was going on around him. When Mark saw him in class after lunch, he seemed the same.

Then halfway through the class, Edward was called to the principal's office. He seemed very confused, though the teacher explained carefully. Mark asked for permission to go with him and the teacher agreed.

In the office, Mark explained to Mr. Marston, "I thought I might be able to

help with the conversation. Edward and
I are friends.''

Mr. Marston motioned for both boys to
sit down. The principal then turned to
Edward. "I'll speak as clearly as possible. I hope you can understand me.''

Edward nodded.

Mr. Marston had Edward's school
folder on his desk. He opened it up. "It
says here that you went to school in San
Diego before you came here. The name of
the school is listed. We checked, and they
have no record of you.''

Edward just stared.

"Do you understand me?'' Mr. Marston
asked. He seemed tense. Mark could
understand how talking to Mr. Velliers
might have upset him. But surely he
didn't believe Mr. Velliers. He probably
just wanted to find out where Edward
Thomas had come from.

Edward shook his head. He looked
around the room. His strange blue eyes
fixed on the view outside the window.

At Mr. Marston's request, Mark tried
to make Edward understand. But

Edward kept shaking his head. He didn't understand.

"Do you know about the sickness here at school?" the principal asked.

Edward nodded. He looked concerned at the mention of sickness.

"Look, Edward, I want to know where you're from," Mr. Marston said. Then he turned to Mark. "The record says he lives with his brother. Will you explain to him that his brother must come to school tomorrow and talk to me?"

Mark relayed the request to Edward. Ed seemed very alarmed. But he nodded and seemed to understand.

Before school was out, the news about Edward was all over school. Someone made a crude sign and posted it on the announcement board.

Edward Thomas is spreading the disease. Edward Thomas must go.

The sign was proof that what Mark had feared was coming true. Sure, most of the kids were treating the "Edward Thomas, diseased alien" story as a big joke. But some took it seriously. Mark overheard some kids saying that the virus was a kind of smallpox. One frightened boy said he heard it disfigured you.

And then, late in the day, Janet Cowley came rushing up to Mark. "Oh, Mark! I just heard that Jody Kendall died! She turned black—like she had bubonic plague—and she died!"

"I didn't hear that," Mark said. "I'm sure Jody is okay."

Mark called the Kendall house. Jody was very sick, but she wasn't dead.

The jokers only made matters worse. Two boys stalked down the halls with red paint smeared on their faces. They rushed at a group of students and screamed, "We got the sickness! The dread disease!"

It was a stupid joke that only added to the strange hysteria slowly swallowing the school.

Mark was glad when the day was finally over. As he headed for the bus, he saw Bill and another boy standing by their motorcycles. They seemed to be talking about something very important. Mark couldn't help but fear they were up to no good.

While Mark stood with Grace waiting for the bus, he saw Sheriff Poulson pull up in his squad car. He called to Mark. "Hi there. I'm here to talk to a boy named Edward Thomas. Is he around?"

"He's gone home already," Mark said nervously.

"Yeah? Well, might try to catch him out where he lives. Wouldn't happen to know where he lives, would you?"

"No, sorry," Mark lied.

"Okay. Well, I'll see him first thing tomorrow then." The sheriff smiled and drove away.

Grace looked at Mark. "How come you lied to him?"

"Maybe Edward wouldn't want the sheriff just dropping in on him."

"Yeah, maybe." Grace looked at the bike rack. "Hey, look. There's his funny old bike. He hasn't gone home at all."

"He's always gone before now," Mark

said.

"Maybe he went to the old apple orchard to study. I saw him there once before. Let's go see."

"Okay," Mark said. "I guess we have time before the bus comes."

They walked behind the school to the apple orchard. The school was pretty deserted by this time.

"Listen!" Grace said.

"What? I just hear the wind," Mark said, listening harder.

"Somebody moaning. Don't you hear it?" Grace said.

"Yeah," Mark said grimly. "Now I do." They hurried between the rows of old trees.

The first thing they noticed was a piece of rope, specked with blood. Then they spotted Edward's tape recorder lying in the grass. It had been smashed against a rock.

"Hey, look—that tree," Grace said.

Mark glanced at the tree. There was blood on the trunk. A heavy black whip lay on the ground beside it.

Mark had seen a whip like that before in the Bryant barn.

"Look at that awful thing," Grace said.

Mark felt sick. He could picture what happened. Probably Bill's dad had gotten mad and whipped him for getting kicked off the basketball team. Bill's dad really loved sports. He would never forgive Bill for ruining the season that way.

In turn, Bill must have been so angry that he had to hurt somebody. So he brought that old whip to school to use on Edward.

"They must have tied Edward to the tree," Grace said. "Look at how the ropes are pulled loose."

"But where's Edward?" Mark wondered. Then he heard the moan again. He rushed over to a broken-down fence. Grace followed.

The boy was lying crumpled in the tall grass. He had been badly beaten. Mark wasn't even sure if he was alive.

"It's Bill Bryant!" Grace cried.

8 THEN BILL GROANED again. His face was bruised, and Mark saw that one of his front teeth had been loosened.

"Look, Mark," Grace shouted. "Larry Dunne is over here!"

Larry Dunne was a good friend of Bill's. They were both on the basketball team, and they went camping together. If Bill wanted to teach Edward a lesson, Larry would have helped him do it.

Larry's face was swollen and his arm was twisted. But he was conscious. When he saw Mark and Grace, he whispered, "Get help!"

Grace ran back to the school while Mark stayed with the boys. "Take it easy," Mark said to Larry. "Grace will bring back help."

"My rib is busted—and I think my arm's broken," Larry mumbled. "That guy—he's a madman. I think he killed Bill."

"Bill is alive. Unconscious, but alive."

"He came at us like a mad dog! He tried to kill us," Larry said. "And for no reason! Thomas is an animal!"

Mark shook his head. "Larry, I saw the ropes and the whip. I saw Edward's smashed tape recorder, too. You guys jumped him, didn't you? You wanted to teach him a lesson, but he turned the tables on you. That's what happened, isn't it?"

Even in his pain, Larry sneered. "You saying I'm lying? Well, it's two against one, Scott.

"Anyway, you should be sticking up for your own friends, not that jerk. He's an outsider. He's not one of us. He made trouble for Bill, and now he's spreading that disease. Nobody likes him. Everybody wants him out of this school."

Larry fell silent when Mr. Marston and the school janitor arrived with Grace.

After checking on Bill, Mr. Marston returned to Larry. "We've sent for the police and an ambulance," Mr. Marston said. "What happened?"

By the time Larry finished repeating his story to Mr. Marston, the ambulance had arrived. Both boys were put on stretchers and taken away.

Mr. Marston watched the ambulance drive away. He looked more grim than Mark had ever seen him.

"It's all my fault," he said. "I should have checked into Thomas' background. Obviously there's something very wrong with him. Now he's seriously injured two of our students."

"I'm not so sure of that," Mark said. He and Grace showed Mr. Marston the broken tape recorder, the ropes, and the whip.

"I think Ed was just studying here," Mark explained. "Bill and Larry jumped him and tried to whip him. I think he was only defending himself."

Mr. Marston shook his head. "Well, I'll check into this, Mark. But in either case, this is the most terrible thing that's ever happened at Marnard. We're not some big city school overrun by violence and vandalism. Eighteen years I've been at this school, and nothing like this has ever happened."

Since the bus had come and gone

without them, Ms. Armstrong drove
Mark and Grace home. The principal had
explained the incident to Ms. Armstrong.
Now she shook her head sadly as she
drove.

"I thought the Thomas boy was ad-
justing quite well, considering," she said.
"He went from an F to a C+ in my class.
Chemistry is hard for most students. He
was doing wonders in so short a time. I
really felt he was a very bright person
slowed down by an unusual background.
I had hope for him."

"I think he was just defending himself
against those two guys, Ms. Armstrong,"
Mark said.

"Just the same, I'm afraid this ruins
everything. Ed Thomas will probably
have to go to another school. Those
ridiculous rumors about the virus being
his fault are bad enough. Now this. Marnard is a small town. People value their
safety here, and they won't put up with
anything that threatens that safety."

At home, Mark and Grace told their
parents about the terrible events at

school. However, they'd already heard much of the story.

Mark's father said, "I understand Sheriff Poulson is going to arrest Edward Thomas."

Mark's heart sank. He pictured the scene at the Marvin place. Edward and his brother would be so frightened.

Then a chilling thought occurred to Mark. There used to be some old guns in the Marvin barn. Perhaps they were still there. In fact, what had Jules used to kill the rabbits that day? They must have at least one gun. And maybe Edward and Jules might be so frightened that they would try to shoot it out with the sheriff.

Just then a car stopped outside.

"It's the sheriff," Grace said.

Mark's father opened the door and invited him in. After an exchange of greetings, the sheriff said, "Hate to bother you folks. Thing is, you probably heard about what that Thomas boy did to two other kids.

"Anyway, I've just been to the place where he and his brother were staying, but they must have run off. No sign of them. I'm told your boy, Mark, was the only friend that Thomas had at school. I'm wondering if he'd know where they might have gone."

Mark stepped forward. "I don't know, sheriff. But I just hope you know that your story is one-sided. There were ropes and a whip at the apple orchard. I think Bill and Larry tried to whip Ed. He was only defending himself when he hit them."

The sheriff smiled. "I'm no judge, boy. All I know is, old Velliers thinks the Thomas boy or his brother probably killed his chickens and beat up Hugh. And I've seen the conditions those two boys live in. Not really what you call normal."

He laughed then. "Folks say they might be aliens. I say they probably ran away from some hospital."

He sighed. "Well, no choice now but to form a posse and catch them before anybody else is hurt."

"Who will be in the posse?" Steve Scott asked.

Sheriff Poulson shrugged. "Most of the good hunters in town."

"Do you want us to come along?" Mr. Scott asked.

Sheriff Poulson coughed nervously. "I don't believe I need any more help right now. If I do, I'll sure let you know."

"I'm sure you will," Mark's father said bitterly.

In about an hour, the sounds of the posse filled the night. Soon the Scotts saw the group come riding past on horseback. Sheriff Poulson led the posse, and his daughter Denise brought up the rear. Bill Bryant's father and Larry Dunne's parents were also riding along. In fact, it seemed that the only ones not in the posse were those who were sick or caring for the sick.

"Looks more like a lynch mob than a posse," Mark's dad said. "Did you see the expression on Bryant's face? That man isn't going to wait for a court and judge if he can help it. He's out for blood."

9 THE POSSE STOPPED right at the Scotts' porch. Sheriff Poulson reported, "We haven't spotted anything yet."

"We sure could use a helicopter with a searchlight," Denise Poulson said. "But even if we could borrow the helicoptor in Springville, no one around here could run it."

"I can," Mark's father said.

Sheriff Poulson smiled that funny smile again. It was how everybody smiled at Mark's father since he had been sick.

"Oh, I wouldn't want to ask you, Steve. You haven't been well and you should take it easy."

One man grumbled, "Those two crazy boys are out there somewhere right now. Probably spreading that sickness all over. My own wife is so sick—might be she's going to die. Yvonne, my kid, is sick, too. She sat right next to that Edward Thomas in school. She brought the sickness home. Those two boys got to be stopped. Beating up innocent people, spreading disease. They got to be stopped."

His eyes glowed with fear. "I remember when there was bubonic plague in the prairie dogs. We had to go out and shoot 'em all. Same thing now as I see it."

"Now hold on," the sheriff said. "We just mean to take those boys into custody. I don't want to hear talk about shooting."

Mr. Bryant patted his long rifle. "Not unless we have to," he said. "But we just might have to." He seemed to enjoy that idea.

With that the posse took off and Mark closed the door. "You're right, Dad," he said. "Something terrible could happen out there tonight."

A sudden look of determination came over Steve Scott's face. He went to the telephone and called Springville. His voice was very calm and businesslike.

"This is Steve Scott from Marnard. Do you remember last year when I borrowed your chopper to get some people out of that brush fire? Yeah, that's right.

"Well, we've got another problem. We have some boys lost in the countryside.

We need the chopper right away.

"Fine. Could you deliver it to the football field by our high school, same as last time? Okay. I'll pick it up there and return it when we're done. Fine. And thanks a lot. This will be a big help," he said and hung up.

Mark stared at his father. "Dad, what are you doing?"

"I think somebody should find those boys before that lynching party does. You heard that man with his talk about prairie dogs and bubonic plague. And you saw the look on Bryant's face.

"I figure I can spot those boys with my searchlight, drop the chopper down, and whisk them away to some safe place. As for paying for the helicopter, let the town do it. After all, they figure I'm crazy anyway. You can't blame a crazy man for pulling a wild stunt, can you?" He winked at Mark.

Mark could scarcely believe it. He hadn't seen his father this excited in a long time. He realized that his father must feel happy just to be doing something useful.

By eleven, Mark's father had driven down to school to check out the helicopter. He'd only been gone a short while when four horses from the posse came galloping up to the front porch.

"I bet something awful has happened already!" Grace said.

The lead rider was Sheriff Poulson. He was carrying somebody in front of him. For a moment Mark thought it was Edward Thomas. Then he realized the body was too short to be Edward's. The body was wrapped in a blanket.

As Sheriff Poulson drew closer, Mark saw that the sheriff was crying. "My daughter! Denise! She's been shot," he shouted.

Mark's mother came to the door. "Oh, dear God!"

They carried the young woman inside the house. She looked as though she were already dead, but she wasn't. The sheriff quickly got on the phone and called the doctor in Springville.

"Doc, my daughter's been shot. Some

fool in our posse saw her standing in the woods. In the dark, he thought she was one of the boys we were looking for—shot her. She's bad, Doc—shot in the head." The sheriff listened for a moment. Then he said, "I'll do my best, Doc," and hung up.

The sheriff turned to them. "Got to get her to Springville. Doc said he can't do any brain surgery here. But it's a long way to Springville. I'm not sure—she might not make it that far."

"Would a helicopter help?" Mark said quickly.

"By the time we get a chopper here, it might be too late," the sheriff said.

"Dad has a chopper now, down at the high school," Mark said.

Sheriff Poulson stared at Mark. "You serious?"

"Yeah," Mark said.

Sheriff Poulson called an ambulance. In a few minutes Denise was on her way to the football field. The chopper was waiting.

In the early hours of the morning,

Mark's father called from Springville. He had taken the injured woman in safely. An ambulance had been waiting in Springville to take Denise to the hospital and she was now in surgery. Everybody was praying for a miracle.

"I'm coming back to Marnard," Mark's father said, "but the sheriff is staying here. He's leaving his deputy in charge of the search party."

Around dawn, Mark's father arrived home. He looked exhausted but happy. The latest word was that Denise Poulson would live.

Mark glowed at the news. His father had saved Denise's life. Without Steve Scott, she probably wouldn't have stood a chance.

With the coming of dawn, the search party began backtracking. Deputy Chuck Jones wasn't as much of a lawman as Sheriff Poulson, and there was a lot of fighting among the posse members.

Twice they circled the Scott farm. The second time they had Velliers' hounds with them. Mark heard the dogs yelping and barking around the chicken house.

"Dogs seem to be on to something," Chuck Jones yelled.

Mark hurried outside. "You'll scare the hens to death if you let those dogs inside. I'll check it out."

"Wait a minute, Mark. That could be dangerous—" the deputy protested. But Mark was already inside.

In a few minutes Mark stuck his head out the window. "It's just an old cat," he shouted to the posse.

Chuck cursed the dogs and the search party was off again.

Mark stood in the chicken house. His legs were numb. He had told Chuck Jones it was just a cat. It wasn't. The dogs knew what they were doing. Hiding in the corner of the chicken house were Edward Thomas and his brother.

Mark stared at the two boys. They both looked scared, like trapped animals. Mark just couldn't betray them.

As the hoofbeats of the posse faded into the distance, Edward stood up slowly. His eyes were wild with fright. His face was bruised and dark. His shirt was gone, and Mark could see where the whip had struck him.

"Don't be frightened. I'll help you, Ed," Mark promised.

Edward opened his mouth. He licked his lips. He began to speak in a strange, nasal voice. "Them go to kill me."

Mark understood now about the tape recorder. Edward was using it to help him learn to speak English. He was not deaf at all. He just spoke another language.

Jules Thomas stood, too. He seemed less willing to trust Mark. He held a long knife in his hand. The muscles in his thick arms bulged like metal straps. His eyes blazed with fear and anger.

"I want to help you," Mark said again.

But Jules didn't understand—or maybe didn't believe. In grim silence, he slowly raised the knife.

10 JUST THEN MARK heard the dogs drawing close again. He knew that this time when they closed in on the chicken coop, the posse would not give up. They would want to look for themselves.

"They're coming back," Mark said. "Please let me help you."

Edward turned to his brother. "He fren—he fren."

Jules shifted his eyes from Mark to Edward and then back to Mark. Finally he put the knife down.

"Follow me," Mark said. He ran to the house, the Thomas boys right behind him.

His parents were shocked at first as Mark explained. Then his father said, "I'll take them away in the pickup truck. I know a safe place. They can hide there until this town calms down."

Mark's mother hesitated. "This is illegal, isn't it? We're taking the law into our own hands."

Steve Scott smiled. "Yes, it probably is illegal. But it's the right thing to do."

Mark's mother thought for a moment, then nodded. "You're right. If that posse caught these boys now, who knows what they'd do. We already had one close call last night with Denise Poulson."

With that, the Thomas brothers got into the pickup truck, and Mark's father sped away. Mark watched them go, hoping his dad knew a really safe place.

Moments later the search party was back. The Scotts poured out of the house to watch. This time some of the posse went inside the chicken coop. All the while the hounds kept yelping.

"You sure those boys haven't been around here lately?" Chuck Jones asked.

"I don't believe so, Chuck," Mark's mother said. "But we've been in the house a lot. Maybe they passed through."

By afternoon the searchers had given up. The Thomas boys were not to be found.

"They disappeared into thin air," one man said. "Maybe they *are* aliens. Maybe they just took off like in the movies."

Most people in town believed the boys

had escaped into another county. They just hoped the Thomas boys wouldn't return.

The next morning, Sheriff Poulson called a town meeting in the school auditorium. A large number of people attended. Nearly everyone who had been sick was much better. Even old Mr. Velliers felt well enough to come.

"The reason I asked you folks to come," the sheriff said, "is to talk about the crisis we had in our town. Real bad crisis."

A murmur of agreement rose in the auditorium.

"I'm happy to say my daughter Denise is going to be okay. They got the bullet out. She should be out of the hospital in a few weeks. Thanks to the good Lord and the quick thinking of Steve Scott, Denise will be fine."

There was a lot of applause.

Sheriff Poulson continued. "I'm going to let Steve tell you the rest of it."

Mark watched his father get up. He didn't seem nervous anymore. He seemed his old, calm self.

"First thing I want to say is, we know the truth about the fight at school. Larry and Bill admitted that they tried to whip Edward Thomas. Larry came clean about it first. Then Bill admitted it, too. So we know that Edward didn't do anything wrong.

"As far as the chicken-stealing goes, well, Jules Thomas admitted that. He said he hit Hugh, but he didn't mean to hurt anybody. The boys were hungry. Mr. Velliers doesn't want to press charges, and I thank him for that."

Mark's father paused and then went on in a strong voice. "I have something to admit, too. I helped the Thomas boys get away when the posse was searching for them. I just didn't think everyone was thinking straight at the time. Some people were so mad they might have done something they'd have regretted later.

"Well, I know helping those boys escape wasn't exactly within the law. But I did what I thought was right."

The audience murmured for a minute.

Then someone began applauding. Quickly almost everyone in the room joined in.

"Last thing I want to say is, seems like the virus was just the three-day flu after all. Everybody is doing fine, and there's nothing strange about this disease at all. I think we ought to be thankful nothing worse happened. I hope we all learned something. I know I did.

"I guess that's about all I had to say. Thanks for listening."

People crowded around Mark's father after his speech. They thanked him for being cool-headed when no one else was. Even his old boss from the insurance agency came over.

"Steve," he said, "how about the best insurance agent I know coming back to work for me?"

Mark's father grinned and said, "You're too late, Mr. Baldwin. I'm going to work for Sheriff Poulson. I'll do deputy work. Should be interesting. I'm really looking forward to it."

Mr. Baldwin smiled weakly. He was disappointed. "Well, good luck, Steve."

As the Scotts headed home after the meeting, they talked about the past few weeks. Much later, out by the stream, Mark got a chance to talk to his father alone.

"I was proud of you, Dad," Mark said. "I've always been proud of you. But the past couple of days really proved to everybody the kind of person you are."

Mark's father smiled. "Thanks, Mark."

"Dad, you didn't say at the meeting, but what happened to Edward and Jules?"

"I took them to an old cabin a friend of mine owns outside of Springville. I told them to stay there and I'd come back and try to help them find a new place. But as I drove away, I saw them heading into the woods. I don't think we will see them again.

"But Edward gave me a message for you. He asked me to thank you for being his friend."

Mark hesitantly asked, "You don't believe for a minute they were some kind of—you know, aliens, do you?"

Mark's father smiled. "Do you think I would admit it if I did? A man with my history of mental problems?"

He shook his head. "More likely they're from across the border. Or maybe they're runaways. Or maybe—who knows?"

Mark was silent a moment. Then he said, "Dad, I read some more of Stephen Vincent Benet after you said you liked him. He wrote some pretty good stuff. You told me one of your favorite lines. Well, the one I liked best goes like this:

Remember that when you say,
I will have none of this exile and this
     stranger,
for his face is not like my face and
     his speech is strange—"

" '—You have denied America with that word,' " his father said, finishing the line.

Mark's father smiled and put his arm around his son's shoulders. "In case I forgot to tell you before, Mark, I'm awfully proud of you, too."